MR. MEN

The Night Before Christmas

Roger Hargreaves

Original concept by
Roger Hargreaves

Written and illustrated by
Adam Hargreaves

It was the night before Christmas, Christmas Eve, and everyone was prepared for Christmas Day.

Everyone except for Mr Wrong, who thought it was the night before his holiday.

All the Mr Men had decorated their Christmas trees, except for Mr Muddle who had decorated himself.

And everyone had sent their letter to Father Christmas in good time, except for Little Miss Late who had only sent her letter that morning.

Would it get to Father Christmas in time?

In each house, the Christmas cakes were baked.

Mr Greedy had sensibly baked three. One for Christmas Eve and one for Christmas Day. And one because you never know when you might feel peckish.

In each house, the stockings were hung by the chimney, in the hope that Father Christmas would soon be there.

Mr Small was not entirely sure it was fair that you had to hang up your own stocking.

And in each house, the presents were wrapped.

Little Miss Naughty's friends were in for quite
a surprise!

The carol singers had sung at each house.

Mr Noisy had loosened some tiles with his 'Ding Dong Merrily on High'!

At the North Pole, Little Miss Christmas had wrapped presents from dawn to dusk, but finally the sleigh was packed.

Father Christmas and Mr Christmas sneaked in a quick cup of tea, waved goodbye to Little Miss Christmas, and then they were away.

But would they stop at Little Miss Late's house?

It was the night before Christmas, and all through the land not a Mr Man was stirring, not even Little Miss Chatterbox. They were all dreaming about a visit from Father Christmas.

Mr Greedy was nestled all snug in his bed with visions of turkey and sprouts dancing in his head!

Everybody was fast asleep. Everybody?

Well, not quite everybody.

Little Miss Late was laying in bed worrying about whether her Christmas letter had arrived in time. And then in the distance she heard the tinkle of sleigh bells.

Little Miss Late jumped out of bed and ran to the window, just in time to see a sleigh and eight tiny reindeer swoop low over her garden.

She knew in an instant it must be Father Christmas.

She held her breath and listened.

The sleigh disappeared out of sight, the tinkle of bells faded . . .

. . . And then grew stronger as Father Christmas and Mr Christmas circled over Little Miss Late's house and glided to a halt on her roof! She heard the patter of little hoofs, the sound of heavy footsteps above her head and knew the letter had arrived in time!

Little Miss Late dashed down to her living room . . .

. . . Just as Father Christmas and Mr Christmas emerged from the fireplace.

Father Christmas was dressed all in red from his head to his foot with a bundle of toys on his back. He took a parcel from his sack and placed it in her stocking.

"And here is something for next year," said Mr Christmas, laying a present beside the Christmas tree. And then with a grin and a wink they disappeared back up the chimney. Little Miss Late looked at the present Mr Christmas had left her.

Can you guess what it was?

It was an advent calendar to help her remember
when to post her letter to Father Christmas next year!